HANGING by Threads

Dear Reader

I have always been fascinated by people and animals who seem to hang by threads.

Bungee jumpers, abseilers, circus performers, rescuers, parachutists, window cleaners and even astronauts all use ropes, wires or cables to keep themselves safe.

> "SPIDERS HANG FROM WEBS AND SPIDER MONKEYS HANG FROM RAINFOREST BRANCHES."

Look closer at bushes and trees and you'll see spiders that hang by threads while they wait for their dinner!

I hope you enjoy reading the stories in this book about people and animals who hang from great heights!

Sharon Parsons

My sincere thanks to the following people for their time, information, images and enthusiasm for this book:

Chapter 3: Victor Hurley, Victorian Peregrine Project, Victoria, Australia

Chapter 4: Lynda and Tracey, Great Heights Window Cleaning, Victoria, Australia

Chapter 8: Chris and Deb Rose, Great Barrier Reef Helicopter Group, Queensland, Australia

Contents

HANGING BY Threads

TEXT TYPE
Information Report

1 Hanging by Threads

Just **Hanging** Around

Glance up and you'll see many people hanging by threads. People use extra-strong threads for all kinds of work and activities in the air.

Spiders not only hang by threads, they are clever enough to make them as well!

Physical Science

Force of Gravity

Gravity is the force that draws objects to other objects. For example, the Earth's gravity draws you down to the ground when you fall.

Strong Forces

When people hang by threads, the forces of wind and gravity can make them move sideways or down. These forces affect what equipment or materials are used to keep people safe.

2 Hanging to Hunt

The **Magic** of Web Weaving

An orb spider weaves a web with silk threads to catch its prey, such as flies. Then it hangs quietly on a thread, waiting for its prey to arrive.

Silk Is Stronger Than Steel

Spider-web silk is stronger and lighter than steel of the same size. Kevlar is the only human-made fibre that is stronger than spider silk.

Threads at Night

Orb spiders often work on their webs at night.

Life Science

Is the Spider Monkey Like a Spider?

Some might say YES! The spider monkey looks like a spider because it has long, slender hands and limbs. It hangs from rainforest branches and rarely comes to the ground.

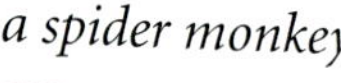

a spider monkey

Life Science

Uses for Silk Thread

Spiders have many uses for their silk thread:

- *for the spiral part of the web*
- *for the straight lines supporting the web and the web's outer rim*
- *to wrap around prey in their web*
- *for females to spin egg sacs.*

The First Thread

LOOK AT STEP 1

Q: How does a spider get the first thread to reach the other side, and make it stick there?

A: The wind helps, and so does some luck!

3 Hanging to Abseil

Rope **Down** Safely

Abseiling helps people go down steep, high places safely. It is useful when people need to get down cliffs, mountain sides, trees or high buildings.

Abseiling for Adventure

Abseiling is also an exciting adventure sport. People can learn how to abseil safely with experienced abseilers.

Not far to go!

Language

What Does "Abseiling" Mean?

Abseiling comes from a German word, abseilen. It means "to rope down". (ab = down + seilen = to rope).

The only way is down!

Safe Abseiling

Abseilers use safety equipment such as strong ropes, harnesses, helmets, gloves, boots and knee pads to ensure they're safe at all times.

just hanging around

"It's cold up here!"

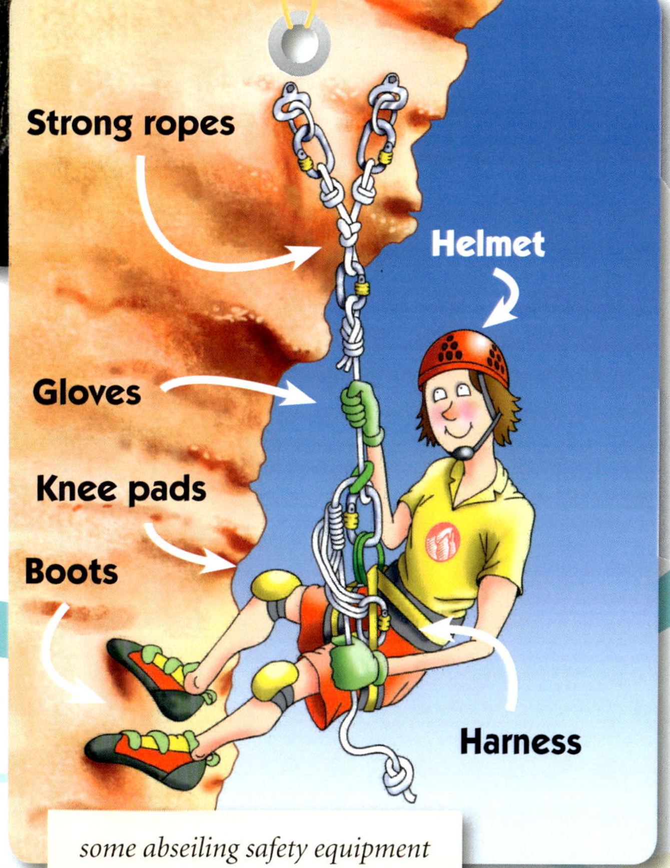

some abseiling safety equipment

Abseiling Aids Chicks

Peregrine falcon chicks watch as their mum flies off to find food.

a female peregrine falcon

Victor Hurley helps peregrine falcons and their chicks. This work is done by abseiling down buildings or towers, or climbing steep cliffs.

Injured Chicks

Victor often gets urgent calls about injured peregrine falcon chicks. Some chicks fall from great heights and are badly hurt. Most of the time Victor can save them.

Abseiling in Spring

Every spring, Victor visits the nests of peregrine falcon chicks in Victoria, Australia. He often has to abseil to their very high nests.

Victor keeps notes on each peregrine falcon. He also tags them. All his work helps more chicks to survive. They are most at risk of dying when they are young.

Abseiling Down Tall Buildings

A peregrine falcon lives in a handmade box on a rocky cliff.

Life Science

Peregrine Falcon

When the peregrine falcon dives through the air, it is the fastest animal on Earth! It does not build nests out of straw or twigs. Instead, it nests on ledges of tall buildings or towers, or in the crags of steep cliffs.

Victor has a long climb up the cliff to reach the peregrine falcon chicks.

Victor abseiled to this ledge on a building 35 floors up to tag the chicks.

4 Hanging for Window Work

Friends **Clean** Windows

Lynda and Tracey are friends who have been cleaning the windows of tall buildings for about 20 years.

After Linda takes her child to daycare, they're ready to start working at great heights.

Abseiling for Work

Most times Lynda and Tracey abseil down tall buildings to clean windows. Sometimes they stand side-by-side on a thick, wooden platform that hangs on strong ropes.

Safety at Work

Safety is the most important part of Lynda and Tracey's job. Every day they check their abseiling equipment, as well as the weather.

On very windy days, the force of the wind can be so strong that it is not safe to work.

5 Hanging to Skydive

A Report on **Skydiving**

Skydiving is a sport where people freefall from a plane for a long distance before releasing their parachute and gliding to the ground. Skydiving companies help those people who want to learn to skydive.

Hanging in Tandem

Beginners often start with a tandem skydive. In tandem skydiving, a beginner and an instructor jump together. They are connected by a harness.

Safety First

Before they leave the ground, new skydivers learn about safety and what happens on a skydive. They learn how to jump, how to use and control their parachute, and how to land safely.

Ready to Skydive

After the safety lesson, it is time for their skydive. First, they are fitted with their parachute and safety equipment. Next, they board a small plane.

Mathematics

Skydive Maths

Skydivers jump from almost 4000 metres high. They freefall for almost 2000 metres, then open their parachutes and drift down for the last 2000 metres.

Freefalling

Jump!

Once the plane climbs to the correct height, a door at the back of the plane is opened. When the skydiving instructor says, "Jump!", the instructor and the beginner jump together.

Freefall

In tandem, they freefall for a long distance. Then the instructor opens the parachute for the last part of the jump.

Enjoy the Skydive

Skydiving instructors are important. They make skydiving safe and enjoyable. Skydiving can be fun as long as people have the proper training and the correct safety equipment.

"LOOK STRAIGHT OUT FROM THE PLANE, DO NOT LOOK DOWN!"

Hanging from Parachutes

Parachutes to the **Rescue!**

People also use parachutes to get to hard-to-reach places, such as mountain tops or remote bushland. Parachutes help rescuers reach people who are stranded and need help.

Physical Science

What a Drag!

A parachute is designed to create "drag". The drag of the air in the parachute slows the descent of the parachutist, so that they land softly and safely.

A parachute creating drag

Parachutes for Spacecraft Landings

Spacecraft use parachutes to help them land safely on Earth after a space mission. The parachutes slow down the spacecraft. They also help the plane to land softly on sea or land.

Technology

From Spacecraft Parachutes to Landing Airbags

In the USA, a spacecraft parachute company is working with the National Aeronautics and Space Administration (NASA) to design new landing airbags. They will work like car airbags as the spacecraft will land on a soft cushion of air.

a NASA space shuttle launch

7 Hanging to Entertain

A **Circus** "Dictionary"

In the circus, aerialists hang from ropes or balance on wires. They entertain us with all kinds of amazing tricks and acts. Check out this circus dictionary for more information about circus acts, equipment and safety.

a trapeze artist

Social Studies

Fly Bar and Catcher

Aerialists swing on a fly bar not a flat seat. The aerialist's partner is the catcher. The catcher is ready to catch the aerialist when they let go of the fly bar.

an aerialist with a fly bar

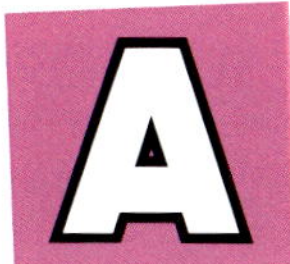

Aerialist: A person who performs circus acts in the air on special equipment such as trapezes and ropes.

Bounce Rope: Like a tightrope wire, except the circus performer walks on rope.

Cloudswing: A large rope in the shape of a "U" that is used for aerial acts – either swinging or hanging still.

Crash Mat: Used by the aerialists to land safely on their feet.

Double Trapeze: A stable, steady trapeze for two aerialists to use together.

Guy Wires: Strong wire cables to support upright poles and other circus equipment.

H and K

Hand Loop and Keeper: Like a foot loop but this one supports the aerialist by the hands. The keeper keeps the hand loop tight.

P

Pulleys: Running ropes through pulleys makes it easier to lift and lower aerialists and their equipment.

CIRCUS

R

Rigger: A person who sets up and looks after the pulleys, cables and equipment.

Rope: A single rope from which an aerialist performs circus acts. The ropes are specially made so they are strong but not rough to touch.

Swinging Trapeze:
A swinging trapeze bar hung from extra-strong ropes.

Tight Wire: A strong wire cable stretched tightly between two points or poles. A circus performer can "walk the wire".

8 Hanging to Help

Helicopters to the Rescue!

Helicopters can take food and supplies to people in hard-to-reach places, such as mountains or bushland. They can hover over a clear area and lower down the supplies.

Helicopter Sea and Air Rescue

Rescue helicopters are used to save people stranded at sea or in high or dangerous places. They can hover over the rescue area and lower someone on a strong rope to help the stranded person. A harness can be attached to the person so they can be winched or lifted to safety.

Helicopters Help for Movies and TV

Helicopters are used to help film TV shows and movies from the air. A movie camera may be fixed to the outside of the helicopter. Sometimes a camera operator hangs from a helicopter to film scenes.

Chris Rose at work

Social Studies

Meet Chris Rose, Helicopter Pilot

Chris Rose is based in Queensland, Australia. His main job is to fly helicopters to film movies and TV shows. One movie he worked on was Australia for Baz Luhrmann, a director. Chris transported the cast and crew to remote areas of Australia for the filming of scenes.

Chris Rose

Index

Glossary

administration	A group of people set up to formally manage and run a project or activity
aeronautics	The use of scientific knowledge to design and build better flying machines, such as aircraft or rockets
cable	A strong cord, rope or wire that is used to securely hold or move something
crags	Steep sections of rock, like those found in cliffs or ledges
descent	Movement from a high place downwards
hover	Staying motionless up in the air
rainforest	Forests with high rainfall, usually at least 1750–2000 mm a year
tandem	Two people doing something together as a pair